Two Ships Passing in the Desert

Short Stories
& A Novelette

Rorry Nighttrain East

DLite Press
P.O. Box 1644
New York N.Y. 10150
http://www.dlitepress.com

Two Ships Passing in the Desert
Short Stories & A Novelette

PRINTING HISTORY
DLite Press/ 2011

ISBN: 978-0-9829774-3-9
Printed in the United States of America

Books & Screenplays by Rorry Nighttrain East

Two Ships Passing in the Desert

Short Stories & A Novelette

Rorry Nighttrain East

To the late Albert H. Vigil
(1919 – 2008)

FOREWORD

As a writer and a teacher of writing, I've developed a sense of writing. In the generic sketches in this work one catches the glimmer of a mind at work in catching the essence of life and transmitting that essence to the page—not an easy task. But Rorry Nighttrain has captured that essence stunningly with a wry sense of life that prompts a concealed smile at the deftly wrought characterizations in the works.

Felipe de Ortego y Gasca, Ph.d.
Scholar in Residence
Western New Mexico University

Introduction

Two Ships Passing in the Desert, was written for our humorous friend Albert H. Vigil, who was still alive in its early beginnings. The overarching theme is that we often just miss connecting with each other−on a daily basis − as human beings.

What I hope to accomplish with this work is to find that certain and triumphant part of us which may have seen this world as a trifle bit crazy and to bathe in the fact that that part of us may actually be correct.

Rorry Nighttrain East
Silver City, New Mexico
January 2, 2011

Table of Contents

10 Two Ships Passing In The Desert

SHIP ONE

FOR A HEART THAT BEARS A CANYON

Whenever I dream of the past, there are still a few unconscious things that try to darken the deepest corners of my mind. Yet, there are so many kindly people around me who just say, "Easy, Pepe." Pepe–that is my name, Pepe Mazon. They always say calm down and take it a bit slower. "You've got a long ways to go."

You see, I run a mystic fruit and vegetable truck stand on the highway en route to the Mimbres river valley of beautiful New Mexico.

The highway leads through some wonderful farmlands and just within range of a cool, winding stream; then it seemingly narrows back into a tight box-fit canyon, even today.

Oh, and a modest dam that was built there in the early 1950's has risen to become quite a serene body of water now called "Bear Canyon Lake." A very striking place in the autumn to be sure, where the leaves of the trees on the farthest shore can turn orange-like and every other yellow-red hue. So alive. It is the sort of place where one might initially think that nothing of any import had ever happened in its depths, except a few days catch of nap, or maybe, a good fishing trip or two. But something did happen there. I remember it so vividly, like it was yesterday, even though a gut-wrenching fifty years had passed. I was a young man of thirty-four back then. It was the 4th of July, as I recall: People were moving about with abandon and celebrating the warm holiday. I thought back to that time when my ex-girlfriend and I were on the far side of a blue lake; yet we were like two ships passing in the desert. For we were talking about breaking-up instead of picnicking, and ...

"Help! Help.... Help!" Came a man's tortured voice from across the rippled lake. "Help. Help!"

"Mamasita? Someone is calling." I jumped to my feet and ran toward the Bear Canyon dam face. "What-is-it? What's going wrong?" I inquired of the young man when I got there.

"I was teaching two teenage girls how to swim and one fell in off the ledge and the other jumped in after her friend and down into the water they both went–down into the deep." He exclaimed in a loosely garbled-tone that made me realize he was probably drunk, or something. "I . . . I tried to dive down there, but–I can't find the girls now. Can you help me?"

At that moment–I just dove down into the chilly waters; it was out of sheer terror or pity, I think, but I was unable to find either of the girls. Then after several tries, I took a breather, and I noticed that the young inebriated man had run off to get the police or maybe to even get the girl's parents. Pensive people had begun to gather in a crowd around the dam's sorrowful face.

A small rowboat with people that had been fishing on the lake began moving towards us and I asked the folks to try and use their fishing lines to snag even one of the girls so that I might swim down while following the line and hopefully bring someone back up to the surface.

"Hey, I've got something!" A fisherman called over from his aluminum boat, in spite of the fact that twenty minutes had already passed. "Okay. Hold it right there. I'll check it out." Pepe said, "That's me, remember Pepe?"' So I swiftly dove down with the line in hand and just as suddenly popped back up with one of the sixteen-year-old girls.

A few people who were on the lake that day now waded out onto a ledge of the dam and brought one of the limp and lifeless girls back to the dry bank. By this time, the drunken boy had returned with one of the girl's parents. The mother was *now* crying something terrible. It was all very difficult to bear.

"Oh. Oh, my poor baby." The mother screamed. "Oh . . . my, my."

"Help me get this girl breathing again," I ordered, as the frantic father suddenly dove into the deepwater for a second girl and brought her up.

"It's no good." I struggled with the words, "A little water has come out of this girl's mouth. It's not enough."

By that point in time, the police and ambulance had arrived just as a few mischievous kids along the lakeshore were setting off firecrackers on the other side, as if nothing had ever happened. I guess they didn't know about the accident. Yet it was then that we gave up on the first girl and we started on the second girl. Things began to look hopeful for a moment when no water came out of the second girl's mouth. Howbeit, no life was left within her.

The policeman that was hovering over us, he just shook his head and quietly said, "She must have died of fright."

"My poor, poor baby," the mother wailed on some more. "She was so afraid of the water." I just looked over at her in sorrow for a second. Then before I knew it, I had already leaped clear up into the rear of an ambulance that was beginning to move away toward the hospital, more than thirteen unlucky miles away.

It had been some lousy 4th of July, so far, for Pepe, I thought. When I finally arrived in the city limits at the hospital it was deemed that there was no more hope left for either of the girls. And I cried.

I was later asked by a policeman about my plans for the rest of the July 4th holiday, and we then both realized that in the mix-up I'd forgotten to make plans for a ride all the way back to the lake. He then drove me. Although, if it had been a lousy day for me, I could only imagine how much more of a lousy day it now was for the girls' relatives. I paused, and withdrew from such alarming thoughts as we safely returned to the lake. For after all, my day had been comparatively wonderful, considering someone had just lost a child in such a helpless manner.

*****

Fifty years have managed to slip by since that flash of two girls before my eyes–and strangely, as if to be some kind of a reprieve from sad old memories. I was working *by* the side of the highway in my retirement and lo and behold; the girl's father; the same man I had seen on Bear Canyon Lake that explosive day so many years ago, now came up to me and said, "Do you remember me?"

"I'm not sure." This now aged Pepe squinted, "You look familiar, sir. Have you purchased some melons here before?" "No. No." The man looked even more deeply into my tired soul, "I just wanted to thank you for trying to help my daughter when she drowned so many years ago."

"I'm so sorry that my help wasn't enough at the time," I had to confess. "Is your wife okay now? Is she at least better?"

"My wife fell sick and died a few years ago. Uh, I think she must have died of a broken heart because she never got over the accident." The man's voice now cracked and quieted. "Anyhow, life goes on, right?"

"That's true" This story-telling Pepe tried desperately to somehow cheer the man. "I'll never forget those girls."

"Well, uh . . . it was good seeing you after such a

long time," said the now daughterless father as he began to awkwardly stroll away.

"Wait. Wait-just-a-minute." I nearly burst a lung. "It seems we have a way of only meeting on the holidays; so I, uh… want to uh… give you some melons and a free pumpkin. Here! These are for Halloween. Take them, please."

"Thanks. B-But why?"

"Let's just say: It's for a heart that has had to bear a canyon." Then the father just ambled away, like that.

I think, that that will be the last time I ever see the heartbroken man a man who once had a teenage girl who left this world for something elsewhere. And well, I'm getting on in years too, eighty-five now, to be exact. So I wouldn't be a bit surprised if those two sweet teenage girls were the first two people that I saw on the other side of the veil, when I get there.

Nonetheless, I suppose . . .even if you'll never get to see our Bear Canyon Lake near the Mimbres River Valley, then this brief remembrance can simply stand for every heart that has ever had to bear the depths of such personal tragedies and such canyons themselves.

THE FIRST BRIDGE TO SPAN THE PACIFIC

ACT 1

Seagulls went flying across the aqua-blue bay, as one lone pigeon fluttered to a stop on the high ledge of an old Victorian house window, in the "City by the Bay", that day. A television warbling in that same room was now interfering with a famous bridge designer's serenity as he squinted his eyes and tried to peer out into the hazy distance toward a legendary orange-looking suspension bridge.

The man was daydreaming about the possibilities of a future earth that was in stark contrast to todays. And in his brilliant mind, he was somehow bridging the now to every single, fragile tomorrow. Though, comprehension and reason were no longer enough; his mind had entered some new realm that only pioneers shared in common. It was a hovering thought–that gravity has to seep through eleven dimensions and that is why gravity is so weak: That's why a magnet can pick up a piece of metal right within the simultaneous pulling-forces of gravity itself.

Then, the TV broadcast won his attention:

'*We interrupt our usual programming for this special news bulletin report. This just in . . . Scientists on a Stanford University research project at the Linear Accelerator have announced their findings in conjunction with a Texas spherical atom-collider. (THE GOD-PARTICLE HAS BEEN*

FOUND.) *Not until this point in history have researchers been able to discover this minute subatomic particle, much smaller than the previously found, quarks and leptons . . .'*

The television set then jumped to an on-location shot of a newswoman, interviewing a local scientist:

"Sir, can you explain in layman's terms, just what this recent discovery will mean to the average person?"

"Well, I'm certain it will mean we will be able to gain a mastery over gravity. Not in the conventional sense, where one might conceive themselves floating off into space, but we will alternate the attract-repel sequences in such a way that objects will now hover at will."

"Is there any more that could come from this uplifting discovery?" she asked in a news-fluffy way.

"Yes. Albert Einstein said that 'Imagination is more important than knowledge.' So, we will be considering all possible avenues for the present and we will cross any other future bridges, ahem, when we get to them. Thank you, ma'am."

" . . . And thank-you. Well, you heard it first, here, on channel 2 news. This is Zookie Tamahara reporting live from the Stanford Linear Accelerator. -Back to you Jim . . ."

*****

The bridge designer's eyes now become 'unglued' from the special news report, as he peered out the Victorian window again and he spoke across the room with a sense of inspiration to his wealthy friend. "Do you realize what this means to the bridge-building community?"

"You can levitate", the wealthy friend joined in. "No more heavy cranes to build those Las Vegas casinos."

"With a variable-gravity formula we could literally lift the mountains of the world into a 'hover mode' and mine the unknown landscapes of the planets beneath," the bridge designer soared. "Think of it."

Just then, he noticed the excellent view of the Golden Gate Bridge, and his wealthy friend made a joke, "Or . . . YOU COULD BUILD THE FIRST BRIDGE ACROSS THE PACIFIC."

"Ocean? Say, you've got something there." The bridge designer now became intrigued. *"AND YOU COULD PUT UP THE FINANCING."*

ACT 2

A groundbreaking ceremony for the new San Francisco to Hawaii Bridge is about to commence.

Men in hardhats were standing under the banner, with a band, and crowds of people and a fanfare of television cameras were strewn about the lower area of the famous Cliff House. As newswoman, Zookie Tamahara began to interview the bridge designer. "Excuse me . . . sir. But I understand you designed the entire bridge. Is that correct?"

"Yes, I did," he exclaimed as he pulled her leg a bit. "All except the trap-door that can be released at-will in the middle of the Pacific Ocean."

The newswoman lost her witty, cheerful composure with, "Ugh, uh . . . what did you say, sir?"

"Just kidding, Zookie . . ." he smiled.

The newswoman tried to sound professional again with, "Just a couple more questions, sir."

"Uh, yes?" He spoke indifferently.

"Of what use could a bridge that takes four days to cross from San Francisco to the Hawaiian Islands, be?"

"Oh, this is much more than a causeway-of-the-continents," the bridge designer beamed again. "It will hover two hundred feet above the sea surface—essentially, flying on its own gravity. It will meet up with the new 'Port-Pacific Manmade Floating Island platform.' An innovative vacation spot. And along its lower length there will be the 'Mid-

Pacific Shopping Mall'—with rest stops, fishing excursions, motels, service stations, two International Youth Hostels; with its eight-lanes of motor vehicle traffic on either side . . . Including, two trains on the bottom deck that will be monitored 24/7 with camera and safety vehicles via the 'Pacific Patrol.' Plus, there will be facilities for all sized ships to dock in safety-harbors during foul weather etc., to facilitate the ship's crews with getting aboard the bridge."

"Can you perhaps dispel a little rumor that's going round?" Zookie Tamahara quizzed. "The word is that there has been a plan-in-the-mix for an Atlantic Bridge project where negotiations fell through at the last moment. Is that so?"

"Yes, that is true," the bridge designer admitted. "It was tentatively planned as a government cooperative between the British Isles and the United States for an emergency Sea Airport to be placed in the mid-Atlantic Ocean: We have established a focus group, which has since come to the conclusion that we should first harness this grand new source of hovering energy, and experiment from a U.S. shore to a U.S. island. Then, we'll consider all the other Atlantic regions."

"Well, there you have it. This is Zookie Tamahara on the shores of the San Francisco Bay, I'm standing near the Bridge Launching Ceremony on my left, of what is sure to become a man-made eighth-wonder-of-the-world in our own time." She reveled all the more in the surrounding excitement.

*****

ACT 3

YEARS LATER...

There stands a gleaming span of colossal bridge-way shooting out over the horizon of which no man or woman has ever laid eyes upon before. It's the first bridge to span the Pacific Ocean, and it has been open for a year; whereupon this magnificent mechanical monstrosity reached out into the infinity of skyline, and mankind's heart, at the same time.

At this very bridge renaming ceremony, the Pacific Bridge is renamed after a great American musician/politician, "Sonny Bono." However, it is subsequently and affectionately nicknamed (THE SUNNY BRIDGE), due to its grand and westward sunsets. A myriad of magazine covers host the "Sunny Bridge" on their covers. PHOTOGRAPHY, SUNSET, YACHTING, & NATIONAL GEOGRAPHIC display their stunning & glorious mid-Pacific sunsets.

"I knew this was going to be big," the bridge designer said, as he waved a fresh magazine in his hand. "But it's always different when the real thing comes along."

"Yeah. It's a great investment I've made here," the wealthy friend replied, zealously. *"So . . . are you ready to drive to Hawaii with me?"*

"Yep." The bridge designer wistfully remarked. "Isn't it funny; you spend almost a generation of time on a project and you're the last one to see your own work."

"Uh-huh, it might have been an entire year since this bridge's opening," the rich friend quipped. "But everyone deserves a little vacation, once in awhile."

"That's true," the bridge designer agreed. "We've worked so hard most our lives. Why should we feel so guilty for taking a bit of exploratory time-off?"

"I wouldn't exactly call this a true vacation," the wealthy friend concerned himself. "It's more of a working-vacation slash bridge-inspection tour."

"Because, we had to leave our poor wives at home?"

"Nah. I'm not even going to dignify *that one* with an answer," the wealthy friend rebuked the point. "Let's go . . . play some real bridge, pal."

At the San Francisco, California bridge entrance, a certain Mercedes with the two industrialist-pioneers, now traveled westward to the sea's horizon until the sleek car simply disappeared at a vanishing point on the bridge's surface.

Later, that same afternoon, the two moguls are seen a few hundred miles out to sea in the fast lane as they whisk past a busy Chevron station.

"Hey, it looks like you planned these distances between gas stations, just right." the wealthy friend said cheerfully.

"Yep," the bridge designer returned, as he now let the streams of fresh ocean breeze comb his hair. "I thought about one or two gas stations every fifty to one hundred miles apart along this bridge, would satisfy most people's gas-thirst and head call needs."

"And . . . you've placed a nice spacious rest stop between the stations."

"Oh, thanks to the new technology, this weightless bridge is a large city with one long Main Street," the designer prided himself. "It's made of an ultra-high-strength non-corrosive future-plastic and our new super-stainless steel."

"Is it true, that if for some reason the 'God Particle's'

hovering ability should fail, the bridge is designed to float?" the wealthy friend now asked while taking in the deep blue shimmers of ocean waters below them.

"Yes, the designer answered."It is calculated into the design for quadrant sections of this bridge to slide downward to rest at the sea-surface so that it may operate at an eighty percent level on a temporary basis.

"What about in storm conditions?" He spied a group of seagulls now clamoring on the bridge's vibrant platinum rails.

"My bridge design will repel the wind with its own stored power, just like an invisible cocoon."

*****

They now drove down an underpass and pulled the car near a gray whale beneath the ramp, where they sat nearby an awaiting and surreal-looking train.

"Yeah, let's see this bridge's underside," said the designer, as he parked in a VIP stall of his own design.

"So this is the famous 'Deep-Water Depot,'" the wealthy friend remarked, at seeing an enormous ocean-liner pass by them.

"It's a French design. One of the fastest yet. This high speed train could get us back to the California mainland in mere minutes," the designer boasted.

"The speed of the train is built-in for emergencies. I thought we'd test it by taking the next milk run to the Port-Pacific Manmade Floating Island, and have the car transported there with us."

"What about dinner, a shower, and maybe even some shuteye?"

"Sure. We can book two sleeper cars."

"Sold. Hey, check out those gray whales down there."

"Yeah. Port-Pacific here we come." the bridge

designer raved. "Maybe we'll even see some big blue whales at the island."

*****

The men rested comfortably in their separate VIP sleeper cars as the train moved over the vast bridge complex through the eerie darkness and high seas of night, until the next morning, when a courteous porter led them off the railcar.

"Good morning gentlemen," the porter called out obsequiously. "I hope your stay on the Port-Pacific Floating Island will be a very pleasant one."

After dropping down several stories in a posh glass elevator, they met up with an aquamarine paradise of verdant palm trees, swaying in a gentle breeze, on a flat-calm edge of sea. A warm yellow sun slowly went waving overhead as the two moguls now hopped into a golf cart for a day on the greens.

"Say . . . this island really rocks," the wealthy man announced.

"Yes. It's run on computer stabilizers powered by solar and wind generated equipment. There's a deep water harbor for cruise ships, and camping, swimming, and even a roller skating rink."

"You've really thought of everything, haven't you," the wealthy pal raved admiringly.

And, by the evening time many hours later, the two adventurous men found themselves on the upper-deck roadway in their Mercedes again—now headed westward, toward the Hawaiian Islands, and road sailing in the direction of an orange and wispy sunset.

"Say Pal, I'm getting tired," the wealthy friend yawned. "How about we take the next off-ramp and crash for the night in one of those bridge motels you've designed and get a fresh start tomorrow morning."

"Sure. Sure. You don't want to miss any of my hi-fi

inventions that I've put into this ocean-hovering overpass."

"Such as . . .?"

"Well, things like my voice-command sheets and self-flushing finger/snap toilets," the bridge designer laughed.

"You really are a techno-nerd aren't you," his passenger chuckled.

By morning time, the bridge travelers began to feel a bit pensive as they started to get back on the road again, while headed out into some foul-looking deep-sea weather.

Clouds were gathering in the west and darkening the daylight so that everything suddenly began to appear strangely night-like.

"Well, it's been a couple of days drive," the wealthy friend hauntingly spoke, with his hidden fear of ocean storms. "How far do you think Hawaii is now?"

"I . . . I can't see the bridge's mileage signs up ahead in all this thick-soup fog," the designer complained.

"Wow, it's really getting bad out here. Look at those mammoth swells, down there, below us."

"Yeah. We'd better take the very next exit off the peak of this erratic link of bridge."

Just then, the Mercedes turned down yet another underpass section, within the cloudburst of rain and threatening sounds about them, where they parked inside a sheltered garage, for a moment.

"Hey, my affluent friend. I think we're going to need a real sudden change of itinerary here."

"What-kind-of-change?"

"We need to split-up," the designer insisted. "I think you'll be much safer if you just take the high-speed train on into Hawaii now, by yourself. Okay?"

"What about you?"

"I'll wait out the storm and finish the rest of my bridge inspection when the skies clear-up in a day or so."

In mere moments, the train had left the lower platform area with the affluent friend and his bridge designer pal was left behind, waving goodbye—as if in a drifting fog-like dreamscape.

*****

ACT 4

Everything has changed, in this dreamscape of moods: The scenery is now even different, and the wealthy friend has found himself standing in a tranquil lime painted hospital room, his head hovering over an ill patient lying prone in a bed. *The man in the hospital bed is the bridge designer!* And there is now a look of terror and frustration, and even a wild-anguish in his contorted face. Because he cannot move or talk. A nurse walks by and softly asks his wealthy friend just how well he actually knew the man in the bed.

"Are you a relative?" she asks, in the present moment, with a slightly unprofessional sense of pity in her voice. "No. No. I'm only an old friend," the rich friend answers.

"I'm new on this hospital wing," the young nurse admits. "Can you tell me what happened to this unfortunate man?"

"He was a brilliant man," the wealthy friend climbed with a new sense of awe and mixed-hurt. "A bridge designer. He came to Hawaii eighteen years ago on just a week's vacation and he called me collect in San Francisco about my possibly funding a new bridge project of his that had never been attempted. But, before he could fill me in me on any of the details, he had a complete and severe mental breakdown. Poor guy. He's been in this vegetative state, ever since . . . ."

"Gosh . . . I wonder what kind of project that might have been?" the nurse whispered.

"I really wish I knew. Knowing him, it must have been something truly grand, and terrific. The 'Pacific bridge' or the 'Pacific-something or other,' was the last he ever said to me."

The bridge designer's eyes were wildly afire as the wealthy mogul and the nurse left his depressing hospital room; but the designer simply wasn't able to communicate with this world anymore. Even though he'd just fully calculated, and invented the first bridge to span the *entire* Pacific Ocean in his mind.

*****

EPILOGUE:

There are those who dream of building and those who build completed dreams. Call them "fantasies," "illusions" or even the "mere chasing of rainbows." Call them what you will. But, when a human being is given a lifetime, they are often the better for having made something good of it.

For example: On this day, one man perhaps saw a bridge too far–but, quite possibly only in his mind; or maybe it even still exists on some ethereal plane somewhere out there on the outskirts and the fringes of hope deferred.

SHIP TWO

HE FELL FOR HER .38's
DETECTIVE SPOOF

CHAPTER 1

PACKING IRON AND BORED

She was only twenty-two, but I had a .38. She was special and so was my way with poodles. Then she simply walked into this man's life like a two-dollar hooker who was giving out twenty-dollar rebates.

Her name back then was Dirty Diane, and she was neither "Dirty" nor "Harry." She carried three .38's with a sheer charm: One was quaintly tucked just under her right arm in a holster, the other was slid into her motorcycle boot, and the last one was jammed someplace that is somehow unspeakable in "G" rated movies.

Oh yeah, and my name is…Jack Hammer. The kind of name that really gets a guy out and pounding the streets. I'm a real Private Eye, you see. A man with a public nose for trouble; and I've got rented earmuffs because the ghetto blasters on my street are murder, she wrote. Ah, but that's another untold geriatric tale.

As you may have already surmised…I don't make a lot of money. The hours are long. The coffee is green–and it's not even decaf–while the donuts are so stale I've often used them as weapons to detain criminals.

It was on a second-floor stakeout that I first placed my private eyes on Dirty Diane's precious .38's. She was inside a dim-lit brick building just across the way, where she had them drawn. Prissy red neon lights just went blinking off and then back on again. As she was doing it. You know: Washing dishes. For she didn't want to get her squirt guns wet. It was then I decided to remain abreast of the peeping Tom . . . I mean, the Detective business in the Golden Gate City by the Bay. So I followed her home that night. Trying not to make a single Jack Hammer noise.

She'd gone all the way, from her late-night restaurant job just off Grant Street in Chinatown to a brisk and windy beach house. It was across the street from the mysterious and serene Pacific Ocean. It looked like a scene from a crime novel.

The old California sun was now coming up, so I ditched my Honda motorcycle by chaining it to a light post and then I went shuffling towards the crab-lined sea, on foot. Ouch!

Once across Highway 1 on the beach I blended in with two bums who were scavenging for aluminum cans at daybreak. All the while, I kept an eye poked over my shoulder towards Dirty Diane's rooftop balcony.

All this was getting me about as far as cement wings on a paper airplane. So I reached into my rucksack and threw a Frisbee over her fence into her side yard and then rang her doorbell.

"Uh, hi there. My name's Jack," I said. "I'm a new neighbor, and I um . . . just accidentally threw my Frisbee into your yard."

"Oh really?" she replied, rather suspiciously, while wrapping herself in a terrycloth robe. "Well, come in and get your stupid toy, mister."

"Oh, it's not just a stupid toy, madam." I peered at her bosoms and almost panted the words out. "It's made of the finest aerodynamic plastics in modern history."

Opening her robe, she says, "And these on the other hand, are just as shapely, and real." She was wearing a pointed brass bra with bolts.

"Where did you get that?" I said.

"Oh, this . . . old thing?" She smiled.

"Yeah, because my grandmother collects antiques and she'd like a post-80's Madonna bra."

She suddenly got angry and says, "You're a copper aren't you?"

"No, madam. I'm not anything near what a penny's made of, I've got more cents."

"Then why have you been following me?"

"Look, I'll come clean lady. I've been following you since last night."

"I know that," she smoldered, and instantly pulled out a plastic .38 special Derringer from a forbidden place. "How did you get that thing up your nose?" I said, with my hands raised high up into the air.

"It wasn't up my nose," she taunted.

So, I said, "then what smells like fish?"

"The maid is cooking salmon patties." She lowered the bantam gun. "You want to stay for lunch mister?"

"I prefer to eat out, madam."

And that was the beginning of our beautiful relationship: Before you know it, we'd set up our own little household and we were both washing clothes together and packing iron, and bored. Holy-monotony style.

CHAPTER 2

BLUED STEEL AND GOLDEN THIGHS

"Oh.... Honey?" I said.

"Yes....my big bloodshot private eye?"

"How much starch do you want in your skirt?" This new domestic Jack Hammer asked her as I pressed her clothes on a frilly ironing board.

"I don't use starch my love," she said as she traipsed by and patted me on the rear as if I were some deflowered slave.

"Do you want to come and back me upon a case tonight?"

"Where is it going to be?" She begged.

"It's on Fisherman's Wharf, sweetheart."

"First – I've got a question." She pouted.

"Yeah?"

"Why do they call it Fisher Man's Wharf? Why don't they call it – Fisher Ladies Pier, or . . . ?"

"Look honey. I need some help. So lose the male-dominated society thing for a second. Do you want to come tonight or not?"

"Yes. Of course, I'll be there."

"Good. Then bring your own blue steel and golden thighs."

"What are you going to bring?" She winked.

"I'll bring the green coffee and the diamond-hard donuts to ward off the bad guys."

"What about your rented earmuffs Jack Hammer?"

"Check. Got 'em."

"And, the . . . poodle?"

"Nah. The poodle stays with the neighbors tonight."

"Oh, I just love you Jack Hammer."

"Love . . . a relative thing."

"Then, I guess I really don't love you Jack Hammer."

"Why not?"

"Because we're not even married."

"See, I told you that love was a *relative* kind of thing." I smirked.

Dirty Diane sighed, "That statement was so dumb, I'll bet you think the word 'KINSHIP' means: 'a boat for getting rid of your in-laws.'"

CHAPTER 3

TWISTED SEX AND A STRAIGHT SHOOTIN' .45

So there we were . . . Jack Hammer and Dirty Diane. Out in the cold night streets. The only male and female holding hands in San Francisco for miles and miles.

It all looked a bit suspicious so we'd detoured on the way to Fisher Ladies. . . . I mean Fisherman's Wharf, and got Dirty Diane a crew cut at a local barbershop.

"How do I look, Jack Hammer?"

"You look like I'm gonna have to call you 'Dirty Dan' from now on. That's how you look."

"But it does the trick, right? We're undercover and I look like a boy, right?" She insisted.

"Yeah. A boy wearing motorcycle boots–with lipstick on."

"I've got an idea. Let's hold hands." She reeled.

"Now, you really do want me to get shot, don't you?"

"No." She now pouted, as we ambled along the Wharf. "So what's this case all about?"

"It's about a woman who's pilfered large sums of money from her dead, rich husband."

"You mean ... murder?"

"Yeah. Murder, by sex, with a dash of intrigue."

"Yes? Well that's not so unusual in this day and age."

"Yeah, but there's a twist to it all."

"What kind of twist?" She plied.

"It's not just your typical murder, slash, grand larceny case." I insisted.

"No?" She tried holding my hand and I backed away. "What is it then?"

"Well, this woman is said to have been working as a dishwasher in Chinatown," I sighed. "So that's how I happened to meet you. I was out late one evening looking for her."

"Then how do you know I'm not your suspect?" She stammered.

"Because she likes twisted sex and she shot her victim with a .45."

"Okay," she softly admitted. "You're fifty percent right about me."

"On the 'twisted-sex' part?" I asked.

"No. I used to have a .45."

"Hey. You would have been really busted back then," I smirked.

Then she shouted, "I still am: I've got two .38's."

Dirty Dan, I mean Dirty Diane, and I bantered back and forth like that for about an hour and a half like a couple of cheap crab cocktails in a five star restaurant; we were out of place, because we really weren't on the menu, and we were both tasteless.

Yet, that didn't slow our resolve to find the murderer. As we took a little ride over to a pawnshop where Dirty Diane picked up her pistola. She asked me if I wanted a bit of twisted sex. Then, I told her to count me out if Chubby Checker was in any way involved.

That's when she shot me! She was a real straight shooter too. Good thing I had my Kevlar jock strap on that evening.

I screamed, "Hey! Why did you just shoot my nasty place?"

"Because I wanted the squirrels to go hungry this

winter." She now snickered with her smoking gun in hand.

"Then you are the woman we're looking for."

"How'd you figure that out?" she wildly laughed. "Did you buy an inkling on the stationary isle at Clue-Mart?"

"Listen lady. You're the one who's bought herself a Pen pal."

"Oh, you ought to be barred from making prison jokes mister."

"Hey, you're going to hear a lot of those kinds of jokes where you're going, lady."

"There's nothing wrong with a little twisted sex and a straight shootin' .45."

"Oh yeah." I stood back up. "I may be old fashioned, but I prefer my women straight and my forty-fives shooting out tunes on an old record player."

"Suit yourself, Hammer." She shot me again in the rear end. Then she ran off into the night streets yelling, "You won't ever nail me, Hammer."

Yes, it's a good thing, I'm Jack Hammer. It was a better thing that I was due to go to the policemen's costume ball as Cinderella, and had my pink Kevlar panties on underneath my jock strap that night.

Though I couldn't help but go over and over her last stupid departing comment: "You won't ever nail me, Hammer;" (I may not have the carpenter gene; but I should have 'SAW' that coming.) I also should have known that the 'pun' is the lowest form of humor.

CHAPTER 4

AT .22 / SHE WAS ALREADY SHOT

The police caught up with Dirty Diane that same night. It just so happens that they were looking for a guy with short hair and motorcycle boots who was wearing coral-red lipstick.

After stopping about eighteen hundred San Francisco residents with that same description that night, the police finally shot and arrested her for impersonating a motorcycle cop. She was now in a lock-up ward at a local hospital and wearing silver bracelets that befitted her charm. So I visited her room, which was posted with one cop wearing eyeliner and the other cop who could have passed for her lipstick-twin

"Oh, uh . . . You remember me?" I said, "I'm Jack Hammer."

"Yes," she sighed. "Just look at me. I'm twenty-two and already shot."

"Sure, but you don't look half as bad as one of those police officers out there patrolling this lock-up room."

"Gee thanks," she cheered. "So what do you think is going to happen to me now?"

"Remember those Pen pals I told you about in the Big House?"

"Yes?" she asked, and she pulled the sheets up over her face.

"Well, some of them will be on the inside of San Quentin, and I'll be one of your pen pals who's on the outside."

"I don't think I can handle prison."

"Well, look on the bright side sweetheart. You've already got the right haircut for it."

"Are you always so encouraging?" she snarled.

"Not usually." I said. "They call me the insensitive detective."

"You know? I may already be shot at twenty-two. But you're just a man with rented earmuffs and borrowed ideals."

"What's that supposed to mean lady?"

"I don't know." She whimpered, "The writer just felt it was time for this story to sound kind of philosophical."

"Oh?" I looked around the room for a second, "Does the author know what my motivation is from here on?"

"I don't know." She changed composure, and now exclaimed fearlessly, "I'll ask, uh ... excuse me. Excuse me, but isn't this hospital scene just a bit maudlin or trite? I mean, if you plan to explore any kind of sensual Hi-fi 40's Detective genre and literature that rises beyond that of 'Dragnet', or even 'Murder She Wrote' wouldn't you want to avoid this crass expenditure of simpleminded sex-innuendos and N.R.A. catch phrases? I mean, I'm not pro nor anti-gun. Nor anti-sex. But clearly, as an author–you will be the first to admit that you are no Ian Fleming. Because hey, we're not doing James Bond here, pal."

"Huh? Oh? What's that? Oh, okay . . . Sure, sure."

Then I asked her, "What did he say, what did your pen pal have to say?"

"The writer just said for us to shut it up or he's gonna make it pretty hard on me in prison."

"Oh yeah? Well, where do we go from here?"

"Well." She smiled wickedly. "I escape from this hospital and you just happen to run into me at a weapon-dealer's house that you've been keeping tabs on in the next chapter. And, uh, you still haven't nailed me, Hammer."

CHAPTER 5

A CLIP JOINT

"Well, well. We meet again, Jack Hammer;" Dirty Diane railed at me from across the weapons dealers' living room.

"Hey, hey, your hair has all grown back." I pounded her. "Now, what kind of bargains do we have here today at Criminals-R-Us? Some exploding toothpaste maybe; a box of Kotex dynamite, or how about that phallic-looking multi-inch barreled magnum you're holding there?"

"It's been a long time, Hammer." She panted.

"Yeah, two years . . . isn't it?" I teased.

"Yes. I'm, twenty-four years old now," she whispered through her empty gun breach.

"Oh really?" I now played on her sympathy. "I remember you once said that I had borrowed ideals, but you were wrong baby. They weren't borrowed."

"Oh yeah?" She pondered slowly through my hazel eyes.

"Yeah. My ideals were rented from a little gift shop down on Pier 31; but how could you have known that."

"Let's ditch this Clip Joint and go have a cup of coffee, Hammer."

"'Sure," I mumbled, "I'm game for having a cup of

java-blend with you; but hold the Irish coffee and stand-up jokes."

So there we were, back together again, after two years of being apart and one hospital escape. Yes, we'd become like a couple of kids with lockjaw who'd just broken into a bubblegum factory as the conversation just went under the table and it got a bit too slobbery and sticky.

"So where have you been all these years, Dirty Diane?" I quietly sipped my coffee.

"Oh, I turned myself in, served my time, and went to private eye school in the Big House."

"Come on. Let's get out of this clip joint." I left a ten-dollar bill and limped away with Dirty Diane to another outdoor bench.

"Now, where were we?" I began again.

"I was telling you that I'm also a licensed private eye." Dirty Diane now spilled her perfume onto my already sore butt-cheek that she'd previously shot.

"Hey. This is becoming an awfully painful conversation," I cringed.

"Well," she brightened. "I'm a real private eye, with a public nose for trouble." Then she drops her fingernail file into my fresh coffee.

"Are you nervous or something?" I pulled the nail file out, dripped the gunk off, and gave it back to her.

"Whatever makes you think that?" She smirked oddly.

"Well, for one thing you keep dropping stuff." I frowned, "and for another, you're using my 'private eye with a public nose for trouble' line."

"Alright." She pulled out a crusty, hardened donut and pointed it straight at me. "Hold it right there. Don't make me use this thing."

"Hey, that's one of my donuts." I stepped back away from her, my hands held high up into the air. "Easy, easy, there. Those deep-fried sugarcoated things are dangerous."

"I know it." She cautiously stepped away from me.

"You know? I wish I'd never set eyes on you, sweetheart," I said, as I nursed a wounded derriere.

"My dead husband said the same thing."

"Is that an admission of guilt?" I prodded her.

"No! I wouldn't hurt a fly." She now kicks a friendly dog that is ambling by, and steps on a cat's tail, and then she pushes an elderly lady off the sidewalk into an oncoming truck and a huge crash is heard.

"The next time we meet you won't get away from Jack Hammer so easily." I now yelled across the bustling street to her.

"Oh yeah?" She still backed away and twirled the rock-hard donut on her finger–then pointed it back at me as if to say, "Who's going stop me? You and which Baker's Dozen?"

CHAPTER 6

HE FELL FOR HER .38'S

I finally ran into Dirty Diane, again . . .

It was later that same year in Golden Gate Park at night, as the saxophones played a haunting melody. Yet we were no longer any good for each other. It seemed the poetry had left our lives. We were no longer like Bogie & Bacall. We were more like a limping Ed Sullivan and a wealthy Minnie Pearl. Yep, the limp in my leg wasn't the only thing that Dirty Diane has left me–limp with. My trouser snake was now more like a micro inchworm who'd forgotten how to use a ruler. Everything had shriveled up, including my Detective ego. For I knew she was only 25; but she was the type that went for huge dangling barrels.

"Hi ya, sweetheart." I called at her in Jack Hammer fashion in the fog. "We had some good times, didn't we?"

"Not that I recall." Dirty Diane fanned the overabundance of fog, just to get a look into my shiny face in the mist. "Do I know you mister?"

"Sure. Sure you know me, my ripe tomato." I announced boldly, with a boxful of donuts just under my arm. "And you're gonna be a vegetable when I get through with you, my sweet tomato."

She suddenly insisted, "But a tomato is a fruit."

"Oh?" I calmed, "Well that mistake was only peanuts."

"Peanuts are a fruit also." She laughed loudly and still tried to clear the fog in order to see me standing there in my tan trench coat and gray-rimmed hat.

"Spill it. What are you trying to say sweetheart?"

"Come on Jack Hammer," she giggled, "First of all: you own a poodle."

"Well, the poodle belongs to the neighbor," I cried. "I only told you it was mine because I thought it would give me some class."

"Okay," she admitted. "Then there's the fact that you live in San Francisco. Fancy boy."

"I'm only here on a job," I insisted. "Again, I just wanted to impress you with some worldly style, I'm really only from Bakersfield."

"Oh?" She sat down on a large rock and the fog cleared.

"You know I almost jumped off the Golden Gate Bridge when we were shacked up and you wouldn't sleep with me. I thought you were a porno star at first, with a suggestive name like 'Jack Hammer.' Then, I went to detective school to try and figure it all out."

"Don't worry your pretty little head," I announced.

"Everybody's so over-worried about sex these days, whether it's the right kind, or whether it's enough, especially in a hot spot like this town. Sex is omnipresent. It's a big joke. Every one of those Baby Boomers seems to insist on acting like little kids who are choosing up teams or something."

"Well, what are you?" She begged me.

"You see what I mean, Dirty Diane?"

"No. What?"

"I'm just a guy who's awkward with women. I'm from the backwoods of Bakersfield, for Moses' sake."

"Oh, yeah?" she muttered, "It sure doesn't take any detective to know that Jack Hammer must have some kind of a preference."

"I do." I replied, as we now hopped onto my golden Honda 350 motorcycle and rode clear over to the Cliff House near an awesome night view of the lit-up Golden Gate Bridge.

"You've been silent all the way over here." She looked well into my detective eyes as the bridge went on flickering just behind us.

"Sweetheart? I'm something that no one ever considers these days." I promised.

"What? What?" She teared up. "I've thought of everything. I thought you were a small barnyard-animal doer. A dead-person perv. Or maybe a bigger fruit fly than even a tomato or a peanut could handle. What? What are you?"

"Look Sweetheart. If I've only learned one thing in being a private eye," I paused for a breath. "It's that human nature sometimes makes people think the worst of their fellow man or woman. I'm not any of those things you've just mentioned. I'm just an asexual guy. I don't mean any disrespect–but I probably make most monks look like super swingers."

"I don't get it," she whined.

"Neither have I. For about twenty years," I then hugged her.

"Oh dear." She whimpered.

"Yeah that's the way it is," I said, as we turned and looked at the Golden Gate together. "With all the diseases and such, I figured I'd find me a new hobby or, at least just wait until I found someone so special that I couldn't resist."

"Too bad, you had the willpower to resist me," she now said, as she almost gave up hope.

"Hey. You're not going to shoot me again are you?" I winked.

"No, no. I just wanted you to bang me." She laughed.

"That's just great, Diane. Because I want you to

know that I love your mind, your great sense of humor in all this. Will you be my girl? Because it doesn't take any kind of detective to realize I've fallen for your .38's."

CHAPTER 7

DEAD DETECTIVES DON'T DANCE

You'll never guess what happened to us. We left the Bay Area and moved all the way back to Bakersfield. (I faked my own drowning in the bay–so no one could trace us). Yeah, and I quit the private eye business too. Because the hours were too long, the fast food was too slow, and my mother said I could have my old bedroom back when I turned fifty. Especially, if I quit using this Bogart accent. *But, it stays, see….*

Yeah. You'll probably never believe this either, but I've got a new profession. Some folks down at the Bakersfield Bakery gave me a job in the donut department. That's because I've always known a lot about donuts and my eyes have been practically glazed-over since the day I was born.

"Jack?" Dirty Diane interrupted me.

"Yeah, baby?"

"If you could be anything else besides a guy who shoots donut holes out of donuts and a cloying detective–what would you be?"

"Oh, I think I'd probably work at the city zoo and be an elephant trainer, Diane."

"Why's that?"

"Because, I'm already used to working for peanuts."

CHAPTER 8

YOU CAN RUN, BUT YOUR PANTYHOSE CAN'T

I later found out that Dirty Diane was a crime just waiting for a place to happen. In my own pedantic mind, I probably thought that maybe she had only committed some kind of misdemeanor of love, or a few infractions of flirtations. Whatever it was it felt illegal, immoral, and fattening.

This former detective hates to admit it, but the donut gig at the bakery didn't work out so I went back into the private eye business. I also discovered that Dirty Diane had a big ugly ex-husband with greasy sideburns who was coincidentally getting out of jail that same week. Yes, in this engagement the cards were neatly stacked against me. I now felt like the bottom card beneath a five-story Hoyle factory: Flat, discarded, and low on diamonds. Of all the luck, I had to pick a girl who was a two-timer. Ah, the facts were clearly before me. Diane was doing the two-guy Tango, like a one-legged dancer on a slick floor. (This meant that she was going to slip-up somewhere.) Or maybe she was more like a blind three-legged dancer in a dirty cat box.

For the crap was not going to wash off so easily this time. Not even with two steam cleaners and one good Jack Hammer. Because my mother once told me that there are only two things in this world that a person can trust: The first one is your instincts, and the second is Mary Poppins. Well, even Mary Poppins is suspect.

I will never forget the day I met Dirty Diane's mean and ugly ex-husband. Wolfgang Biter was his scrappy name. Yes, Dirty Diane had run away from Bakersfield all the way up north to the Marina District of San Francisco and it was just to be with that paroled jailbird. A devil's-cage cretin.

"Jack Hammer, I want you to meet Wolfgang Biter," Dirty Diane boasted on that dreadful day.

"Um, how are you?" I coolly returned.

"I'm parole bored," he snarled back at me.

"How interesting." I waned. For all this double-action stuff had gotten way too fast for me. I was now determined to drop Dirty Diane. I was going to drop her like an Ex-lax candy bar in an acute diarrhea ward.

CHAPTER 9

THE TRUE CALIBER OF HER LOVE

"Quick! Hand me some bullets!" Wolfgang screeched as he shot into the city streets at me.

"Whatever are you going to do with them?" Dirty Diane gulped.

"It's open-season on private detectives and I haven't met my quota yet."

"You can't shoot Jack Hammer," she cringed. "You'll have to buy two deer-Tags and a new Trout Stamp. We just cannot afford that."

"Oh, phooey. I knew there was something fishy about that guy," Wolfgang complained.

Little did Wolfgang Biter know, that I, the famous Jack Hammer–yes, I had snuck into their bathroom and overheard their entire conversation. All of this while Wolfgang was shooting at a mannequin decoy that only looked like me. So I dashed into their kitchen, grabbed an empty coffee cup, and then threw my own special blend of green coffee into his face.

"AAAAHHHHHH!" Wolfgang gagged and spit, and he tossed all around the room. "What is this stuff?"

"It's Jack Hammer's homemade mace." Dirty Diane growled, as I slipped out the side door and down the street, making good my escape.

I was now down one two-timing girlfriend and a place to live. Thus, I began sleeping in my old vacant office building on a crusty potato chip-laden vinyl sofa.

It was late, one night a few weeks later, when a knock came upon the door-glass, as the SanFran fog drifted in through an open window. All I could see was the vague silhouette of a woman's figure. Her body swiveled as if she was some kind of joy ride at the local amusement park. It was Dirty Diane.

"I've been lookin' for your address all night–Hammer." She sauntered up to my desk and sat on it.

"Why? Is your ugly ex-husband going to mail me a bomb?" I shivered without letting her know.

Just then she pulled out a .357 magnum and pointed it at me. "You've missed your big chance to get on Wolfgang's Xmas mailing list, pal."

"How about for old time's sake–you let me go." I played on her sympathetic side, "And I'll forget about all the charges the coppers have on you."

"No-can-do my ex-Detective boyfriend." She almost softened in the heat of the moment. "Wolfgang is going to want to see a body."

"That's easy my-love. Show him yours." I winked, "And we'll just have to tell him we had .357 reasons to part company."

"No." She screamed.

I just knew, that when we first met, I should have made like a pair of nylons–and run.

*****

It was a good thing for me that Dirty Diane had cleaned up and gotten rid of her dirty image. It was even more astounding just how much of a bad influence Wolfgang Biter had been on her after all these years. Yet, when she turned him in on a parole violation and then came back to me, the City had become a better place for we fugitives of love.

"What did the cops get old Wolfgang on?" I pried.

"Oh, they initially took him in for a misdemeanor," she answered softly. "But now he's in for grand theft Spam."

"You know: Relationships should be a misdemeanor," I spoke quite seriously.

"Oh, really?" She chuckled.

"Yeah. The more a guy can't find his Miss, the meaner he gets."

"I'm sorry, I shot you in your lemonade-stand-maker, Jack." She teared up, "But those were the old days."

"Yeah?"

"Yeah," she sighed. "I plan to steal your heart back, if I can."

I smiled back at her and said, "Isn't that grand theft Spam or something?"

*****

I've got me a new office down in Oxnard now. (Oxnard-Hoooonnnkk. Wrong answer!) Yeah, it's kinda fun dealin' with all these wanna-be movie stars near Tinsel Town. I sure have some crazy cases these days too. Why just the other night I told a new client,

"So, let me get this clear. You say your wife just made like a pair of nylons—and ran?"

"Yes," the client answered me in an embarrassed tone.

"Well, she can run, but her pantyhose can't—mister."

"What's that suppose to mean Mr. Hammer?"

"It means that wherever there is any kind of pseudo-violence or corny-sex-intrigue; the creator of this detective series will have me sittin' in some dank and musty old room of some flea-bitten motel and I'll probably be watchin' the same tiresome TV detective . . . show . . . reruns in my filthy underwear."

"I still don't get what you mean." The client insisted.

"That means I will have really grown as a person." I shouted like a blaring Jack Hammer out into those hardened law-broken and cold night streets.

CHAPTER 10

FUNERAL FOR A CLUE

Due to financial reversals at my Oxnard Detective Agency, Dirty Diane and I, the famous Jack Hammer, were forced to move back to Bakersfield, California, to open up a new office in my old bedroom at my mother's house.

I was really beginning to think that P.I. stood for either "Poor Idiot" or "Person Inept." I didn't have a funeral for a clue–what life was about. Oh, but I did finally nail Dirty Diane: You see, my mother had asked me to repair some loose boards on her front porch, and .... (I may not have the carpenter's gene; but, how do you work them dang nail guns anyway?)

That's when I was handed an unsolved overload case from some other neighboring detective agency called Pinkerton's. It was a real messy job, man. I had no idea that there were hags with exploding colostomy bags. They were roaming all over Bakersfield and making a mess in rest homes, intensive care units, and now they were even leaving dirty trails up and down our once fine streets. However, my Jack Hammer instincts told me that there was a stinky underlying plot to corner the air freshener market by introducing their stench upon our sensitive noses. Yep, I was sort of right.

I'd traced this messy plot all the way to a seriously

radical gal named "Ann Archy." (Just like the word that means utter confusion.) She was a militant-pacifist. Still, her mother who made machine gun soup was the only lead I had on her. It was even said that Ann Archy had a kind streak in her because she helped her mother get off welfare by running Clorox-filled squirt guns for rowdy preschoolers down in Colombia. Well, maybe she was meaner than she was nice because she'd let her mother teach her how to manufacture exploding pre-filled colostomy bags in order to make it out on her own. It was only sometime after the fact that I finally realized that the cleaning solvent and perfume industries would not be able to cleanup such a vast mess, and that such companies were willing to pay a handsome price to have it all just go away. This was Operation Sponge Bath. That's where I came in.

"So, you are Ann Archy's mother?" I questioned a mean-looking elderly lady, who just happened to have a Thompson machine gun strattled across her lap.

"Yeah Hammer," she said as she spit a wad of tobacco into a wide spittoon beside her rocking chair. "Keep it short. I'm overdue to an underwater basket weaving class tonight."

"You're lying!" I shouted.

"So what?" She jousted back at me.

"I just want to know where your daughter is . . . " I argued back at her sour-wrinkled face.

"She's over at the Tampax Dynamite factory," Ann Archy's mother cried.

"Why are you telling me the truth? Is this a trap?"

"No. No. I just realized that I should have raised my mean daughter better," the old woman sounded. "I should have sent her to the Girl Scouts and taught her how to do underwater basket weaving so she'd have a trade. Say, it's not too late for you to rescue her, is it?"

"Nah, it's not too late." I, the great Jack Hammer blasted. "I think I can save her from herself; then I'll reindoctrinate her back into society as a fully-equipped mindless person who'll wander about like a lost child under all the duress of our lying and manipulative politician's phony rule."

"Oh, that's a mouthful." She stammered.

*****

The next thing you know, I had Ann Archy cornered in a rustic and abandoned Tampax Dynamite factory.

"Hold it right there." My powerful Hammer voice echoed across that vacant building, as I held a shaky firearm pointed at her. "Your mother wanted you to be a Girl Scout so stand up, and show us your cookies."

"I've got a better idea," Ann Archy sneered.

"What's that?"

"I've got a box of Nitro Glycerin Douche Bags here with a timer on 'em set to go off in five minutes." She craftily bargained.

"So?" I laughed, "What's the worst thing that could happen? Is it gonna wash my vagina breath away?"

"Hey," she raved, "I've got thunder-douche in my arms and you're makin' stupid jokes at a time like this?"

"Alright. Okay. I'll give *you* a four minute and forty-nine second getaway lead time." I then dropped my sweaty weapon.

CHAPTER 11

CAR CHASE WITH A BIKINI AND A BAYONET

Oh, did I forget to tell you? Ann Archy was wearing a bikini with cowboy boots, and a black stovepipe hat, when she got away from me.

We must have sped around that curious neighborhood for hours. Back and forth. People just stood on their lawns scratching their heads a bit, as one mad woman flew by, waving a shiny bayonet into the air from her convertible and cussing at me. All this while she tossed her douche bags out and hit a few bystanders. Yes, Ann Archy fought me off for quite a while, but I kept her shapely body in my trusty night-scope and eventually caught up to her.

"Alright . . . now, get out of the car." I demanded.

"Hey, but you don't even know me Jack Hammer." She pouted, with her hands held up in the night air.

"Well, as sure as I know that P.I. stands for 'Potential Ignoramus' – I know *you.*"

"Just what do you know?" She stalled.

"I know your favorite color is 'infrared.'"

"How-did-you-know-that?" She winced.

"Your mother, who makes machine gun pie, told me." I barked.

"You? The famous Jack Hammer believed a story like that, from an old woman who makes exploding colostomy bags?" She quizzed me. "Besides, she doesn't make pie she makes soup."

"Well?" I stammered back in my best detective style, "Now that you put it that way–she could have been lying to me."

"Whew, now you're getting it Hammer. My mother played you like a cheap violin."

"So, what was a nice girl like you doing in an abandoned Tampax factory, anyway?" I lowered my black-painted water pistol filled with Clorox.

"I was, uh . . . looking for a place to store all my Girl Scout cookies." She slightly fidgeted.

"Lady, how do I know you're on the level?"

"First–you tell me how a double dummy like you ever got in the detective business." She pulled out a hidden Nitro Glycerin Douche Bag and pointed it right at me.

"Easy there, baby-doll." I backed away.

"How's your feminine hygiene doing, Hammer?" She now poked me in the chest with that dangerous plastic thingy.

"Okay. Okay. Look, I'll admit I'm a stupid detective, on my bad days. It's only sometimes though."

"Sometimes . . .?"

"Alright. All the time," I croaked in fear.

"Good-bye Hammer. See you when they hand out the next merit badges for inept private eyes." She blew a kiss and I never told anyone till now how I goofed up on that case. Because the last I heard – Ann Archy was down in South America with her dear old mother and they were studying underwater basket weaving with that crazy thug– Hugo Chavez. I didn't get paid for that gig either. Well, not if you count the sixty-day stint I did in a mental lock-up ward for suggesting to the ten o'clock news that someone was trying to corner the perfume market by simultaneously exploding millions of colostomy bags and creating a fresh-air shortage. CASE UNSOLVED.

CHAPTER 12

P.I. STANDS FOR PRETTY-MUCH INDIGENT

It was beginning to look like I would be living at my mom's house in Bakersfield for a long, long time. That is, if P.I. stood for 'Pretty-much Indigent.' My detective reputation was ruined. Oh, it seemed that I, the legendary and celebrated Jack Hammer was now a permanent momma's-boy and general houseguest. It was humiliating. For she was now giving this fifty-plus-year-old man detective advice.

"Jack Hammer." My mother pulled me by the nap of the neck and over to the sofa. "You know, I'm with MADDD now."

"Mad Magazine?" I asked.

"No. I'm with Mothers Against Doubly-Dumb-Detectives." Mom Hammer cried.

"Oh?" I laughed, "Do you know any dumb detectives?"

"Now look," she shouted. "Your father may have raised you to be a nitwit and a fool, but if you want your old bedroom back you are going to listen to everything I have to say."

"Oh . . . Do you know where dear old dad is?" I groveled.

"You're the detective." She admonished me, "You go and find him."

"H-Huh?" I stuttered.

"Don't you see, Jack Hammer?" Mom Hammer cried, "You are truly a 'A#1' dumb detective."

"Why would you say that?" I calmly asked, and then sat back on the sofa twiddling my thumbs and wanting to play a game of marbles.

"For one thing, you keep returning to this house." She worried aloud, "Oh, I know you've had your heart set on being a great private detective since you were a little boy, but . . ."

"Yeah. Yeah?" I ate some stale old popcorn from under the sofa cushions. "Yeah, mom?"

"B-But my son–you really stink at being a private eye."

"I can't be that bad." I shook in my seat.

"Ah, you're total crap son." Mom Hammer insisted, "I mean you royally suck at it."

"How bad am I at it, mom?"

"Enough to make me want to be president of Mothers Against Doubly-Dumb-Detectives, son."

She'd given me a lot of sage advice that day. Yes, my mother also mentioned that I had super-bad judgment when it came to picking women to date, although I already knew that. For I now had a girlfriend named Dirty Diane, and that wasn't exactly a girl-next-door puritanical name. Then, there was "Easily Dunn", a gal who had traipsed up to me, down south on a Ventura beach, and she said: "Hi, I'm Easily Dunn, mister–how about you?" Now, she was a real winner. Yeah. She was pretending to scam senior citizens for their Social Security checks in games of checkers and chess on the wharf. Yet when I found out that Easily Dunn was actually an undercover cop I felt like a long walking detective on a short pier. She even tried to arrest me for being The WeakWhitePawnRapist, although I had a great alibi: I was on a date with Easily Dunn when the rapist last struck. It was of course, my last date with her. Yes, I, Jack Hammer, the ever fascinating-and-super-sexy-private eye, the pure envy of all other detectives, was a cheap excuse for a vintage lady's man. A man with one foot stuck in the '40's and the other shoe doing a rare proctology self-exam.

Yes. I was now a true super-loser. Me, Jack Hammer, with my royal scepter in hand (the toilet plunger). Oh, the detectives' jaded crown of all crapolla was now mine, all mine. Waaa, Waa!

CHAPTER 13

CHILD OF A LESSER GUN

I was always jealous of my older brother Mike (that's the great 'MIKE HAMMER'), and then there was the fact that he had an excellent author behind him–like Mickey Spillane. You see, my older brother was always the true success of the family, and I was only a black sheep. I had always been like a Hammer on someone's thumb.

Yeah, every Hammer has to claw his own way to the top. So I went up on a San Francisco apartment rooftop and began to contemplate my career as a private eye. I felt picked-on, bullied by the system, and pushed against the wall by forces unseen. I felt like for the first time in my life there weren't enough Dirty Diane's, nor Dirty Harry's, nor enough hours of green coffee (the moldy kind), to get me out of this mental jam. Oh, I could run but my pantyhose couldn't (figuratively speaking). I felt like life's "G-spot" no longer stood for gun. It was all now one big shootout on Port-a-Potty Lane. For, I was truly a child of a lesser gun. Yep, I was going to finally find another line of work, anything but detective work.

"Jack?" Dirty Diane asked me later on that same evening.

"Yeah."

"Are you serious about wanting a real job?"

"Of course—I am," he mumbled.

"Well, just to show you there are no hard feelings, Wolfgang Biter says in a letter here that he knew you wanted to be an elephant trainer so he had his father send you this job application—for the San Francisco City Zoo."

"He did that from San Quentin?"Hammer cried.

"Sure." She said, "He likes the way that you've typed-up your whole life story and that you are so prolific, and he was just wondering if you'd be his new pen pal?"

"I'll have to think about that one, my love."

"Well, ugh . . . What about the job at the city zoo?" She bantered on, "You'll even get to start with the penguins."

"Then, this looks like the end of the line for my fabulous private eye career," Jack moaned.

"Yes, but you'll be moving upwards—Jack."

"How's that?" He still didn't have a funeral for a clue.

"Just think. All your co-workers will now be wearing cool skintight tuxedos."

Most folks probably won't be too surprised to find out that I goofed up on my job at the city zoo by putting laundry detergent in the penguin's swimming water, and that twelve-foot pile of suds can still be seen circling Alcatraz Island, so they say. I wouldn't know—because I was fired and instead of moving back to Mom Hammer's, I drove past Bakersfield and all the way to New Mexico.

Dirty Diane came to Silver City about a year ago on a bus, but our little fling didn't last. She went nuts. It all happened sort of slowly. Everyone here thinks she just got too enchanted. But we were always like two ships passing in the desert. That's just the way it was with us. Perhaps we should have never met.

Although, it was only the other day that I ran into my humble next-door neighbor and friend while shopping downtown. Mrs. Garcia and I began this conversation:

"It's really busy downtown this morning," Mrs. Garcia said in her usual happy, smiling manner. "Don't you just love our 'land of enchantment?'"

"Yes," Jack Hammer answered. "There's a real swarm of people out here today–it's like a March sandstorm of them."

"I even saw Diane just a moment ago. You know Dirty Diane, don't you Jack?"

"Yeah, I used to date her. But it didn't work out."

Mrs. Garcia paused with a heavy-heart, "Poor girl: No mamma. No papa. No money. No Jack."

"Yes, it's sad that she's gone all the way back . . ." Jack flatly stated.

"Gone back?"

"Uh-huh," he sighed. "She's gone all the way back to her old ways of being lonely in the swarm."

"There's an old Spanish saying about such people," Mrs. Garcia almost cried the words out.

"What is it?"He painfully asked.

Mrs. Garcia whimpered, "The saying goes: 'THEY ARE NOT DEAD WHO LIE PEACEFULLY IN A COLD TOMB; BUT DEAD ARE THOSE WHOSE SOUL IS DEAD, AND YET THEY ARE WITH US DAILY.'"

- Finis -

ABOUT THE AUTHOR

Rorry Nighttrain East a.k.a. R.L. Farr is truly a literary-anomaly. At least, he's really some kind of author to try and typecast, nor even place into any single mode or genre. For he seems to run all the gamuts of poetry and prose, screenplays, teleplays, humor, short stories and even novels. What's next from this versatile new talent? He says he writes because he's handicapped, and we believe him. (With two artificial legs thrown in, to boot.) Always a surprise. Read him, then re-read him. Laugh, cry . . . and wipe the tears away. You've found yourself the pen pal of a lifetime. Born on July 18, 1952 in Fresno, California, he is an alumnus of De Anza College Cupertino, California, and was formerly a journeyman automobile mechanic for a Lincoln Mercury dealership in San Jose, California. He has since moved from "the Golden State," and he now resides on a ranch where he writes in the beautiful mile-high mountains of Silver City, New Mexico.

ABOUT THE BOOK

TWO SHIPS PASSING IN THE DESERT is a book of short stories woven into a diminutive sized novelette. A theme of raw living runs through its pages as its chapters are filled with a subtle sadness and a plethora of insane humor. (It describes in detail, just how we miss each other as fellow human beings – on an everyday basis.) Reads like a fast-paced novel. It is tender, funny, engaging, and moving.

FREE PREVIEW

HE FELL FOR HER .38's (Detective Spoof): "She was only twenty-two, but I had a .38. She was special and so was my way with poodles. Then she simply walked into this man's life like a two dollar hooker who was giving out twenty-dollar rebates . . . " "How'd you figure that out," she wildly laughed. "Did you buy an inkling on the stationary isle at Clue-Mart?"

Contact Us: DLite Press.
Email: info@dlitepress for author's information